Barney,™ BJ™ and Scooter™

PUFFIN BOOKS

Dear Parents

This is a simple story about all that is involved in properly caring for a pet. Caring for a pet is an excellent way to help teach young children a sense of responsibility. BJ learned that it is both fun and hard work taking care of a pet.

We consider books to be lifelong gifts that develop and enhance the love of reading. We hope you enjoy reading along with BJ!

Mary Ann Dudko, Ph.D.
Margie Larsen, M.Ed.
Early Childhood Educational Specialists

Art Director: Tricia Legault
Designer: Hilarie Brannan Ireton

PUFFIN BOOKS

Published by the Penguin Group under licence from Lyons Partnership, L.P.
Penguin Books Ltd, 27 Wrights Lane, London W8 5TZ, England
Penguin Books USA Inc., 375 Hudson Street, New York, New York 10014, USA
Penguin Books Australia Ltd, Ringwood, Victoria, Australia
Penguin Books Canada Ltd, 10 Alcorn Avenue, Toronto, Ontario, Canada M4V 3B2
Penguin Books (NZ) Ltd, 182–190 Wairau Road, Auckland 10, New Zealand

Penguin Books Ltd, Registered Offices: Harmondsworth, Middlesex, England

First published in the USA by Barney™ Publishing, a division of Lyons Partnership, L.P. 1995
Published in Puffin Books 1997
10 9 8 7 6 5 4 3 2

Barney, BJ and Scooter

Written by Mary Ann Dudko, Ph.D. and Margie Larsen, M.Ed.
Illustrated by Bill Langley

BJ is taking care of his friend's puppy, Scooter.
BJ is very excited.

BJ knows that taking care of a puppy is a lot of fun,
but it's hard work, too.

Every day BJ needs to feed Scooter.
Scooter is always hungry.

He eats lots of puppy food.
Scooter is growing bigger and bigger each day.

Every day BJ needs to give Scooter a bowl of water.
Scooter is a thirsty puppy.

The cool, fresh water tastes so good.
Sometimes Scooter drinks two bowls of water.

Every day BJ needs to take Scooter for a walk.

Scooter likes to walk and run with BJ.

Every day BJ plays with Scooter.
BJ enjoys playing with Scooter.

Scooter likes to play ball.

Every day BJ needs to let Scooter take a nap.

Scooter is a tired puppy.
He sleeps and sleeps and sleeps.

Sometimes BJ needs to give Scooter a bath.

BJ is ready with a towel, but Scooter shakes himself dry.

Sometimes BJ needs to brush Scooter.

Scooter is a shiny, clean puppy.
Doesn't Scooter look handsome!

Sometimes BJ needs to take Scooter to the vet.

Scooter is a healthy, happy puppy.

BJ knows it's a lot of hard work taking care of a puppy,
but it's fun, too!